Tiny Rabbit was
a very lonely rabbit.

He had no friends, no books to read,
no games to play and lived alone in
a tiny house on Tiny Island very far away.

At the back of Tiny Rabbit's tiny house was the most beautiful garden. It grew tiny carrots, tiny cassavas, tiny cabbages and tiny yams.

Each morning, Tiny Rabbit watered his beautiful garden and each day he hoed and ploughed the land.

At the front of Tiny Rabbit's tiny house grew some of the island's most amazing flowers. There were tiny hibiscuses, tiny frangipanis and tiny periwinkles.

Tiny Rabbit loved flowers and would sit alone, among the flower beds, to savour their sweet smell.

One bright sunny day, Tiny Rabbit woke up, hopped out of bed and yawned a great big yawn.

'Well,' thought Tiny Rabbit, 'it's about time I find myself some friends. I have lived alone much too long.'

But the only animals for Tiny Rabbit to make friends with were the ones in the neighbouring villages and the nearest village was three miles away.

Poor Tiny Rabbit! He would have to hop all the way.

After having a tiny carrot for his breakfast, Tiny Rabbit set off alone on his long lonely hop. He took with him, in a basket, a tiny cabbage and a tiny yam.

He HOPPED and HOPPED and HOPPED, passing TREES after TREES, WOODS after WOODS.

As he came to a patch of land covered in guava trees, he heard a loud tiny cry.

'HELP! HELP! HELP!'

Tiny Rabbit stopped and listened. He listened very carefully. It was the cry of Tiny Bird. Tiny Bird had caught one of his tiny wings amid some brambles beneath an old-looking guava tree.

Tiny Rabbit rushed to his rescue and set him free.

'THANK YOU. THANK YOU,' said Tiny Bird lamely. 'I don't know what I would have done without you.' And he flew away before Tiny Rabbit could utter a word.

Tiny Rabbit was very annoyed. He sat down upon the brambles beneath the old-looking guava tree and began to eat from his basket.

Soon, Tiny Rabbit was fast asleep. He SLEPT and SLEPT and SLEPT.

And do you know what time Tiny Rabbit woke up? The next day at the crack of dawn!

'Oh dear,' uttered Tiny Rabbit as he listened to the faint crows of tiny roosters and the faint cackles of tiny hens, 'I must have fallen asleep.'

Poor Tiny Rabbit! He did not know what to do. Should he return home or should he continue on his journey?

'Well,' thought Tiny Rabbit feeling rather disappointed with himself, 'I shall return home to water my garden and to hoe my land. Who cares about friends anyway?'

And, without a book to read or a game to play, Tiny Rabbit returned to his tiny house. But he was not alone. There to meet him, at the front of his house, sat Tiny Bird, the little bird that he had helped.

HOP, HOP, HOP went Tiny Rabbit with a smile on his face.